An Unofficial Roblox Story

Diary of a Roblox Hacker: Nobody's Fool

Volume 2

Authors:

K*Spicer and

Little Walker

Published by Kristina Walker and
JMW, LLC Company
8924 E Pinnacle Peak Rd, Ste G5-109
Scottsdale, AZ 85255 USA

Table of Contents

Chapter 1

TGIF

John Doe's Diary Entry #1:

JACK,

WHO USES THE WORD DIARY? SOUNDS DUMB. I LIKE JACK. HI JACK - AGAIN.

NOW THINGS HAVE SETTLED AND TIME HAS PASSED. BET THEY THINK IT IS OVER. HA!!) SILLY NOOBS!!!

THIS IS JUST STARTING TO GET FUN. WAIT UNTIL THEY START TO FORGET ABOUT ME. THIS TIME I HAVE FRIENDS WORKING THE SYSTEM TOO.

THEY WON'T KNOW WHAT TO BELIEVE ANYMORE. TICK TOCK... AND PART TWO OF MY WRATH BEGINS!!!

JD

SEE YA LATER JACK!!

Friday, March 31st, at KSpicer's house two weeks after "the incident."

FaceTime connects.

Child321654: Can you play?

KSpicer333: Yeah. I'm in Minecraft.

C: Still too chicken to play Roblox?

K: Really? Look who's talkin' ya chicken noob.

C: NOOB? I'm not a noob!!! A noob in what?

K: Bed wars.

C: Oh right! I can kick your booty any day in Bed Wars!!! You are the worst at that game!

K: Alright chicken little noobie pants, then let's play. I dominate!

C: HA! Let's do this then. Solo, no teams.

K: Join my party.

C: No, I'm MVP+. I'll ask you for a party.

K: Fine. Let's pay that mushroom world one.

C: Mushroom world...yeah, I know what you mean.

5 minutes later...

C: I see you building up.

K: So?

C: Just sayin'.

K: It's just us and green. What is he doing anyway?

C: Who knows.

K: I'm going to go destroy his bed.

C: Cool. Too scared to come get me?

K: NO! I'm just getting him out of the way so we can battle.

C: Uh huh.

K: Whatever. Hey, where is he?

C: I dunno, mid?

K: Nope.

C: Destroying your bed? (Bursts out laughing)

K: Hilarious! No, not there. I was just there. Checked the spawners...nope. Weird. Where is this guy? I'm headed to his base again.

C: K.

K: YES!!! Destroyed his bed!!! Where is this dude? I'm after you green!!!

On the chat:

BLUE'S BED DESTROYED

C: I told you to check your own base, son! HAAAAAAA!

K: UGH!!! No, I was just there! How did he get there? There's no way! It was surrounded by obsidian!!! That's it, I'm getting this guy and then it's just you and me.

C: You're never going to destroy my bed. I'm the master at this. Come and get me.

K: Where is green? This guy is making me nuts! I'm after you BeastBoy.

C: Maybe he's a hacker.

K: Not a hacker.

C: Maybe it's John Doe...

K: Stop it! Not funny. Is he near you?

C: Nope. No one can get into my lair.

K: Lair? Really? What are you a dragon? Or is that just your bad breath I smell?

C: You are just hilarious. Ha Ha.

K: Stink breath. That's your new name.

C: Funny not funny.

K: Wait, I think I see him at mid. You are mine beastie!

KSpicer suddenly screams out loud.

K: Not fair!!! That scared me!!! Where did he come from? He cheated! So NOT fair! I saw him at mid. How did get behind me?

C: What? What happened?

K: I DIED!!!

C: Well I know that. But how?

K: I don't even know! He was at mid!!! I swear I saw him!!!

C: Maybe he is one of John Doe's minions, out to get you.

K: STOP IT!!! That's NOT funny! I told you never to bring that up.

C: Maybe BeastBoy is Guest666's best friend and they are targeting the famous KSpicer!

K: Seriously, stop it.

C: Ah, there's green. Come to me greenie and watch him die. Oh BeastBoy, are you John Doe's BFF? Want to jump through my screen and come get me? Or are you only after KSpicer?

K: STOP!!!!

C: What the what? Where did he go? It's like he disappeared.

K: SEE...I told you!

C: Come here you hacker! I'm going to knock you into the void. Come get me and I'll give you KSpicer!!!

K: Seriously? You're so dumb.

C: Sudden death is in 30 seconds!

K: I'm AFK for a minute.

C: NOW? But it's sudden death! You're just jelly.

K: I'm not jelly! BRB!

C: Fine.

Chapter 2
ROBLOX HAPPENS

30 minutes later.

KSpicer333: I'm back, what happened?

Child321654: Where were you?!? It's been like five hours!

K: It hasn't been five hours, drama queen.

C: Well it's been forever.

K: I went to the bathroom and then my mom needed me.

C: I bet you were just constipated.

K: I am not! Gross! My mom did need me.

C: Uh huh.

K: What ev's. So, what happened? Did you win?

C: Almost! BeastBoy is super sneaky. I bet he cheated.

K: Oh Really?

C: Anyway, I got bored waiting so I moved to Roblox.

Long pause.

K: Oh.

C: Come on, join me!

K: No, that's okay. I think I'll just watch some YouTube.

C: Are you ever going to play Roblox again?

K: I will, I'm just not ready.

C: Seriously, you know that there is no way that John Doe is really after you. It was all a big hoax remember?

K: Oh yeah, I remember! TOO well. CutiePIe's cousin Brian was standing right next to you when I got the phone call. Do YOU remember that part? If he pulled off the hoax then who called my mom's phone?

C: Who knows!?! It was probably his roommate or something. I'm sure they thought it would be pretty sweet to keep the John Doe thing going.

K: But Brian said he had nothing to do with the phone call and you know it! You were there. You heard the whole thing just like me. Don't tell me that you weren't completely freaked out that night too. You were with me and I know you were just as scared as I was.

C: I still think it was Brian's roommate. Think about it. Do you really think that the guy that hacked into the famous John Doe account is actually after you?

K: I dunno. It feels like it.

C: It was just CutiePie, Brian and his buddies. I'm sure if it!

K: I guess. I'm still just completely freaked out.

C: Let's just go into Roblox together and play something that isn't scary. No Murder Mystery or Hello Neighbor, or anything remotely terrifying.

K: Ya think?

C: Okay, so what is the complete opposite of a scary Roblox game?

K: I have NO idea.

C: What about Robloxia High School?

K: Nah, too many people.

C: Come on! That is the best place to be!!! So many other people for John Doe to bother. Just kidding.

K: I'll only play if I pick the game. AND if you stop mentioning John Doe.

C: FINE! I'm okay with that. I actually just want you to play again.

K: I know, let's get our own server and play Tix Factory. I'm about to be reborn for the fourth time!

C: YES!!! I just got reborn for the fourth-time last weekend. It's amazing. I can't wait to have one tixilion dollars...

K: Lol.

John Doe Diary Entry #2:

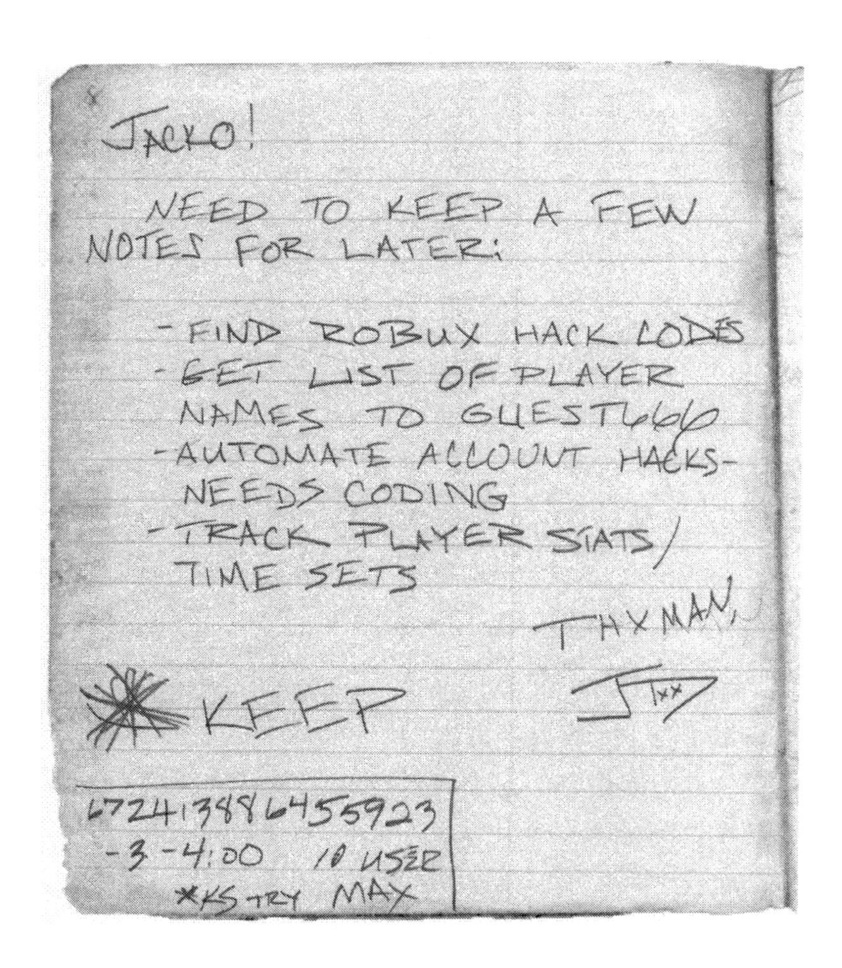

JACKO!

NEED TO KEEP A FEW NOTES FOR LATER:

- FIND ROBUX HACK CODES
- GET LIST OF PLAYER NAMES TO GUEST666
- AUTOMATE ACCOUNT HACKS- NEEDS CODING
- TRACK PLAYER STATS/ TIME SETS

THX MAN,

J TXX

* KEEP

6724138864559 23
-3 -4:00 10 USER
*KS TRY MAX

Chapter 3

VAMPIRE'S BRING BAD LUCK

The next morning at 10:35am. KSpicer FaceTimes Child321654.

Child321654: I'm with CutiePIe.

KSpicer333: Oh hey!

CutiePie55: Hey K! I'm at CC's.

K: Cool. What are you guys playing?

C: Robloxian High School.

CP: I heard that they are adding fidget spinners soon! I login every day to see if they made the update.

K: Okay, random.

C: In real life, my new fidget spinner will be here any day. I ordered the galaxy one! I cannot wait!

CP: I've seen that one, it is pretty cool. I just got the glow in the dark one. It is SOOOO awesome.

K: Alright people, focus! Back to Roblox, please.

CP: Ooops, sorry. I'm just obsessed, that's all.

C: Me too! Did you see the Musical.ly about the fidget spinner?

K: Uh hello...Roblox??? That's weird, why am I not logged in?

C: Oh yeah, sorry. See? I told you I was obsessed.

K: I see that. So, who wants to play Treeland?

CP: No way. I can't do that game.

C: Why?

CP: I don't know. It's hard for me so it's not that fun.

K: Hard? How is it hard?

CP: Hey CC, did you tell KSpicer what happened this morning?

K: Nice way to change the subject. Tell me what?

C: No, let's not do this.

K: Wait, what? Why not? What are you talking about?

C: Um, never mind. Let's just play Tix or something.

CP: Oooo, yeah Tix! I'm almost reborn.

C: Reborn for the first time?

CP: Yeah, Tyler told me about it.

C: I've already been reborn four times!

K: Are you two serious? Is no one going to tell me what happened this morning? I'm still right here ya know. It's not like I forgot already.

CP: Oh, it wasn't anything big.

K: Really? Then why did you mention it and now won't talk about it?

CP: Just came to mind, that's all.

K: Liar! Tell me or I'm not playing!

C: Fine, fine, I'll tell you. But you have to promise me you'll play Tix with us.

K: Now you're making me nervous. What? What happened?

C: Promise me first! That you'll play.

K: Okay fine, I'll play. Now tell me!!!

CP: I'll let CC tell you.

C: Okay...thanks for that.

CP: No prob.

C: Ugh! So, I was playing Vampire Kingdom...

CP: We.

C: Yeah, WE were playing Vampire Kingdom this morning when CutiePie first came over.

K: Uh huh.

C: Um, and, well...

K: Yeah, go on.

C: Well, I mean it was weird because it didn't feel like the same map as usual but we played anyways.

CP: It was cool because it seemed extra creepy.

C: Yeah and we had just watched a YouTube video with Tyler reading a Hooked story! It was such epic timing!

CP: I know, right? We couldn't have planned that!

K: Okay okay, I get it. You two are completely off the rails again.

C: Oh sorry. But it was epic, just sayin'.

K: Got it! Get to the point!!!

C: K, so we were playing and we came up to this John Doe statue that people were talking about, which was pretty funny. He had these vampire teeth with blood and it was hilarious looking. I mean, his dumb noob face with vamp teeth. Classic. Wish I had made a screenshot of that!

K: Again, going off topic.

C: Yeah, so we were standing there. And all of the sudden in the chat, JD pops up.

CP: And we thought it was part of the game, so we kind of ignored it.

C: Yeah, so then we realized that it was the real chat because...

Long pause.

K: Because?!?

C: Ummmm....

K: Somebody better start talking!!!

CP: I should probably go now.

K: NO WAY!!! WHAT HAPPENED?!?!

C: Well, JD...(whispering)

K: What? I can't hear you!

C: JohnDoeaskedwhereyouwereinthechat!!!

K: What do you mean?

CP: We were just playing and JD came up in the chat and actually typed, "Where is KSpicer?"

FaceTime Ends abruptly.

John Doe's Diary Entry #3:

JACK MAN,

NOT MUCH TIME.. RUNNING A FEW TESTS. THIS MUST BE PERFECT B4 I GO FULL FORCE.

WHY DO I LOVE FREAKING THESE KIDS OUT SO MUCH?

A LITTLE HERE, A LITTLE THERE, LIKE BREAD CRUMBS. JUST ENOUGH TO KEEP THEM INTERESTED THEN...

WHAM

CANT WAIT!

LATER,

Chapter 4
WHO'S THE FOOL?

FaceTime rings at KSpicer's house. KSpicer sits, staring at the iPad, heart pounding, tears forming. FaceTime continues to ring.

Inside KSpicer's head: This cannot be happening! No way, this isn't real. Am I dreaming? This is a nightmare!!! What did I do to deserve this? Why me? Why is John Doe after me? It's not like I did anything to him. I'm not even a hacker. I don't even have 500 Robux! What am I going to do? Maybe it's just dumb ol' Brian and his hacker friends. Let's hope so. Calm down, it has to be Brian again. Maybe... I hope so...

Finally, KSpicer answers. Child's and CutiePie's faces appear with huge smiles.

Child321654 and CutiePie55: APRIL FOOLS!!!!!!!

KSpicer333: WHAT?!? (gasping)

CP: Its April Fool's Day fool! Gotcha!!! You totally fell for that and it was all my idea! (Starts laughing hysterically)

K: That is so MEAN!!! Not cool, NOT cool!

CP: It's not mean, it's April Fools! Can't you take a joke?

K: I thought I was going to have a heart attack!!! You know I'm still freaked out about all that. That is not cool, not cool at all. That is not what friends do.

C: Sorry K, we didn't think you would get mad. And I almost backed out and said we shouldn't do it!

K: REALLY? And I thought I could trust you, CC. Of all people!

CP: It was totally my idea, don't blame CC.

K: Yeah, but you both pranked me. That's it! I'm banning you both from my server FOREVER!!!

C: Oh, come on! Please don't do that, we're really sorry. I thought you might freak for a second, but then I thought you would think it was funny. At least a little funny.

K: Well it's not!

CP: Yeah, I'm kind of getting' that vibe.

C: You always love pulling April Fool's jokes, so we thought we would prank you first.

K: Anything to do with John Doe is not funny. Not funny at all! You know how I feel about that right now. Too close. Way too close to laugh about.

CP: Okay, okay, I'm sorry too. Gotta leave, going to the movies.

C: Okay, bye Cutie!

CP: I'll call later. Bye.

CutiePie leaves Child's house and heads home.

C: You still there?

K: Yup. Not happy.

C: Sorry K. Wanna play?

K: Not really.

C: Wanna watch YouTube videos together?

K: I dunno, maybe.

C: Musical.ly?

K: Not in the mood.

C: How about something completely different?

K: Like what?

C: Want to come over?

K: I dunno. Why?

C: I have an idea.

K: What is it?

C: Want to prank CutiePie?

K: YES! I'll be right there!

KSpicer ends FaceTime, jumps off the bed and races down the street to Child's house.

John Doe's Diary Entry #4:

JOHNNY J- (TRYING THIS OUT. LET ME KNOW IF YOU LIKE IT. XX)

ITS OUR DAY IF ALL GOES AS PLANNED. APRIL FOOLS!!!

LET'S JUST SEE WHO IS THE BIGGEST APRIL FOOL, IT'S LIKE FISHING. BE PATIENT AND SEE WHO BITES.

NIBBLE NIBBLE LITTLE NOOBS...

GOTCHA!!!

$2T ROBUX SCHEME IN ACTION

*CODES ONLY →

Chapter 5
PRANK ON THE BRAIN

DING DONG DING DONG DING DONG.... Child opens the door. KSpicer flies into the house bursting past Child, completely out of breath.

Child321654: Whoa, that was fast! I hardly got from my room to the kitchen before the doorbell rang. I guess you really want to do this prank!

KSpicer333: Yeah DUH! (still panting)

C: I was going to say, "come in" but clearly it is too late for that.

K: Yeah, sorry. Just excited.

C: I see that. Want some food?

K: No thanks.

C: You sure? I'm getting some tortilla chips.

K: Big shocker. No, I'm good.

C: Water?

K: Yes, please.

C: I think we need to bring in the big guns for this one.

K: What are you talking about?

C: We need to have help to pull off a good prank on CutiePie. You know, like parents or Brian or something?

K: No, not Brian, never Brian! I, you know, "H" that guy.

C: Whoa, pretty bold! Don't say that - you don't "H" anyone. You're just still mad at him. Which I get. But Brian is actually a pretty cool guy and super smart too. I know you would like him if you got to know him. Had he not been the one to terrorize you and all, ya know?

K: Yeah, I do know! That's the problem.

C: It wasn't like it was his idea or anything. CutiePie is the one that started it. He just pulled off the technical stuff.

K: Whatever, don't remind me.

C: Okay, so Brian's not your first choice. What about asking our parents?

K: Our parents aren't going to help us pull off a prank!

C: You never know, we could ask.

K: My mom would just get mad and give me some speech about being nice to others and stuff. Not appropriate, blah blah blah...not asking.

C: Well mine might help. But we have to come up with a plan first.

K: Really? They would help?

C: I bet they would! You know how much I love April Fool's Day. And my dad gets pretty into the pranks. Who do you think I got it from?

K: Hmm. What could we pull off while CutiePie is at the movies?

C: Not sure, but we do have ALL day you know. April Fool's Day goes until midnight.

K: True. And CutiePie does like to stay up late...

C: Okay, let's think about what scares CutiePie the most?

K: I have NO idea. Wait, are we doing an online prank or a real-life prank?

C: Either. Both. IDK. Whatever we think up that is the best, I guess.

K: This has to be really good, ya know? Something we will laugh about for years!!! I mean CutiePie does deserve it after this morning.

C: (Bursts out laughing.) You were pretty scared! I wish I had been in your room to see your face.

K: You just think you're so funny!

Child continues to laugh. KSpicer finally joins in.

K: Okay, I admit, I was petrified! I couldn't move an inch and I just sat there. I think I almost pee'd my pants!!!

Child and KSpicer burst out laughing even harder.

C: I might pee my pants right now!!!

Child runs off towards the bathroom.

John Doe's Diary Entry #5:

J-DUB,

"MONEY MONEY MONEY MO-NEY"

HOURS AWAY AND TAKING NAMES. THE WAITING IS MAKING ME CRAZY.

GUESTL66 AND MY SECRET WEAPON ARE ALL IN. WHO IS GOING TO ~~BE~~ NOOB ENOUGH TO PLAY MY GAME? THIS IS ALL TOO GOOD. THEY WONT BE ABLE TO RESIST!!!

AHH THE WAITING IS MAKING ME ANXIOUS....

ALL WORK AND NO PLAY MAKES JD A DULL BOY

*TEXT G63 THE USERS THAT TAKE BAIT BY 7:00

-JD IXX

Chapter 6
IPAD TROUBLE

KSpicer and Child work furiously on ideas to punk CutiePie. Although some of the ideas are incredibly tricky, they find it difficult to come up with something that they can possibly be pulled off in one day.

An iPad rings, but it isn't KSpicer's or Child's. Child checks the hallway, searches under the desk, then searches under the bed and finally spies CutiePie's iPad under the poufy marshmallow pillow on the bed.

KSpicer333: What the heck? Whose iPad is that?

Child321654: CutiePie's! I guess she forgot it when she left so quickly for the movies.

K: Well well well, isn't that just convenient for us!

C: Yea, right? (Looking a bit nervous.)

K: Here, hand it over. I can't wait to set her up big time.

C: Maybe we shouldn't. I mean that would be too obvious, right? Maybe we should do something that she won't expect once she realizes that the iPad is here.

K: It doesn't have to be obvious!!! We just need to get in there and mess around a bit. This is brilliant.

C: I think we should leave it alone and do something else completely outrageous.

K: What are you talking about? We have been trying to plan this for hours! Now we finally catch a break and you want to back out?

C: I didn't say I was going to back out!!! I said we should just maybe do something different. Without the iPad.

K: What is your deal?

C: Nothing, not a deal.

K: Here, hand it over. I promise I won't do anything without you agreeing.

C: No, I better give this to my mom or I might get in trouble.

K: Okay, now you are just acting crazy. Hand it over...

C: No!

K: HAND IT OVER!

C: NO!!!

K: Oh, I get it, I forgot to say the magic word, right? Real funny! PLEASE, hand it over.

C: No, I'm just going to give it to my mom and we will do something different. I promise.

Child heads towards the door. KSpicer leaps across the room and grabs the iPad from Child's arms. Child shrieks and almost falls backwards on the floor. KSpicer hops over Child's body and starts for the door. Child grabs KSpicer's leg and tries to stop her and get back the iPad. KSpicer pulls away with a twist and flies out into the hallway and rushes towards the bathroom.

Child trips and lunges forward out the door reaching the hallway just as the bathroom door slams. And locks. Child bangs at the bathroom door furiously.

C: KSpicer, STOP! This isn't funny. Put down the iPad!!!

K: What exactly is so important on this iPad that you don't want me to see?

C: Nothing! It just isn't ours and we shouldn't mess around with it.

K: Oh really?!? That sounds like you. Since when haven't you wanted to touch someone else's iPad? Especially to pull off an epic prank?

C: It's just that...

K: Uh huh... (Typing in CutiePie's password.)

C: Just that...

K: Yep, still listening. (Starts flipping through open apps.)

Child sits in silence, dreading what KSpicer is about to discover.

KSpicer breaks into an instant sweat. Knees crumble slowly and falls to the ground, still holding onto the iPad with a death grip. Tears are starting to form and only a whisper can be heard.

K: Please tell me this isn't real.

John Doe's Diary Entry #6:

JAKEY J,

YO!

I BET THEY ARE WETTING IN THEIR BABY NOOB DIAPERS. WHO IS GOING TO BE MAN ENOUGH TO PLAY???

R.O.F.L!

WHY IS THIS SO FUN? AND THE BEST IS YET TO COME, AM I RIGHT J?

*KEEP

RED + BLACK ARE MY FAVS

J xx

I ROCK!!!

Chapter 7
MASTER PLAN

KSpicer333 sees the Party Request from John Doe along with Guest666.

Child321654: Please open the door, K.

No response.

C: Please? Please open the door so I can explain.

KSpicer333: Was that really an April Fool's joke?

C: Please, just open the door! I will tell you everything if you would just open the door.

5 minutes pass. KSpicer unlocks the door. Child jumps up and turns the handle. KSpicer is white as a ghost, just staring at the iPad in disbelief.

C: I'm sure this is just Brian and CutiePie continuing the prank. Probably their way of pulling the ultimate April Fool's joke.

KSpicer sits quietly and nods.

C: You know CutiePie, always wanting to get away with the last laugh.

K: The message this morning from John Doe WAS real, wasn't it? He really did ask about me!

C: Well, it did happen when we were playing, but I think CutiePie had something to do with it.

K: Why would it come up on her screen in Roblox? Wouldn't she have just done it to me?

C: Yea, well, I mean...I just think it is part of a bigger prank. A master plan! CutiePie wasn't sure when you would play Roblox again and maybe this was another Brian move.

K: Really? Do you really believe that? Why did you prank me with this as an April Fool's joke earlier?

C: CutiePie said she was going to tell you and we argued. I said we couldn't do that to you and needed to just forget about it. Then she had to go and bring it up on FaceTime! So, I made her say April Fool's when we got back on.

K: And you still think this was all a prank?

C: I really don't know. Maybe it was an April Fool's joke CutiePie had already planned? I don't want anything to do with this!!!

K: Then why did you lie to me?

C: I didn't lie! I just...just didn't tell you the whole story.

K: Another way to lie.

C: I'm so sorry, I really was just trying to protect you! I didn't want you to get scared again. Just as everything was settling down. I mean, I finally got you to play again and everything!!!

K: You should have told me.

C: I'm sorry…it was a bad call. I still do think that Brian may have something to do with this and it could still be CutiePie's master April Fool's Day plan.

K: Doubt that. I mean maybe, but I really doubt it.

C: Can we just focus on a new plan to get CutiePie? Just to lighten things up?

K: Lighten things up? LIGHTEN THINGS UP?!? John Doe is still after me!!! How am I supposed to "lighten things up?"

C: Thanks for the air quotes. And if you think about it, it isn't actually John Doe because some unknown person hacked into the Roblox Admin's John Doe account years ago. And…

K: Really? Are you really going there? I know John Doe isn't a real person, but whoever took over the account IS a real person. So what difference does it make? Someone, as we now call John Doe, is targeting ME!!!

C: Fine, I get it, I'm sorry. I just really don't know what to do. Should we tell your parents? My parents? We have to do something! We can't just sit here and be scared all day.

K: Let's go to my house.

C: Okay, great! Good plan. Let's leave the iPad just in case CutiePie stops by.

K: Fine. I don't really want to see that screenshot again anyways.

Child helps KSpicer up off the floor. They slowly make their way over to KSpicer's house, stopping occasionally to kick rocks or point out something meaningless. They both seemed to be stalling for time.

John Doe's Diary Entry #7:

Chapter 8
BASKETCASE

15 minutes later, the two make their way into KSpicer's house.

Child321654: I got it!

KSpicer333: What? You got what?

C: The most brilliant idea ever!!!

K: Lay it on me.

C: Huh?

K: I dunno, that's what my dad says when I have an idea. Okay, tell me.

C: Okay, weird. Anyways, here's the plan... Use ME as bait.

K: WHAT?!? Why would you do that? And honestly, I don't get it.

C: Lol.

K: What exactly do you mean by bait?

C: What if I somehow try to get John Doe to troll me and then we can have Brian shadow my computer and do his techno magic. Then we can find him for real and call the police!

K: Call the police for what?

C: I don't know. Okay, we can do that only if he really IS a stalker.

K: Um, okay. But I still don't get it. What the heck is techno magic and why would John Doe go after you? Why wouldn't we just have Brian shadow MY computer instead since apparently JD finds me anywhere?

C: Oh, that's a good point. Sounds much easier too. And better for me.

K: You've been watching too many horror vids on YouTube!

C: True story. I'm totally addicted.

K: So, are we back to no plan? And what does this have to do with pranking CutiePie?

C: True. And I really have no idea. It pretty much has nothing to do with CutiePie and was the only thing that popped into my head! Give me some credit at least for trying!

K: Credit given. Now, I think we need to FOCUS.

C: Me? Not focused? LOL! I do have an issue... Let me grab my fidget spinner. It helps me think.

KSpicer rolls eyes.

K: Uh huh, sure it does...

FaceTime rings on KSpicer's iPad.

C: Basketcase87? Who's that?

K: Never heard of 'em. What the heck?

C: Answer it!

K: Um, no thanks. I'll pass.

C: Seriously!!! Answer it!!!

K: Not happening!

C: Be brave, let's finish this thing once and for all.

K: What?!? NOOOOOOO!

Child shoves KSpicer over and answers the call. KSpicer starts to freak out, dives onto the bed, and throws a blanket over her head.

C: REALLY K? What are you three? You poopy McScotchy!

From the iPad: Hey that's my line! And who's the poopy McScotchy?

KSpicer immediately sits up and throws off the blanket.

K: You're the poopy McScotchy!!! What are you trying to do, give me a heart attack? Who is Basketcase87 anyways? Why would you DO that?

CP: Whoa whoa whoa!!! Slow down, K. I was just calling to find out if you have seen my iPad. I think I left it at Child's this morning. I called Child first and then you. So obviously I can't call you from mine!!!

K: Well duh!

C: So, who is Basketcase87?

CP: Oh yeah! (Starts laughing) That's my grandma's username. I'm using her iPad since I'm at her house.

K: Really? Basketcase? That is SO not a grandma's name...

CP: Swear!!! My mom came up with it since my grandma is a basket case at using technology. My grandma thought that was hilarious and went with it. And she is 87 years old, so there is that. Gotta love her. She stinks at technology, but she's a good sport.

Everyone burst out laughing.

C: You're lucky she even has an iPad!

K: Right?!?

CP: So. what are you guys doing?

K: Coming up with a way to prank you.

CP: Wait what?

KSpicer and Child exchange glances and start laughing so hard that they can't speak.

CP: What is going on? What's so funny? Come on guys!!! Let me in on it! Prank me? For what? Oh, come on!!!

KSpicer finally blurts out: Okay okay! Whew, that was just hilarious. I could NOT stop laughing!!! I will let Child fill you in while I recover here. My stomach is killing me from all that.

Child begins to fill in CutiePie on all that went on since CutiePie left in the morning.

John Doe's Diary Entry #8:

JACKSTER,

I AM THE ROBUX MASTER $$$

WE ARE ALL SET. I KNEW G6³ WOULD COME THROUGH. I WISH I COULD SEE THEIR FACES WHEN THE BAIT GETS SET.

HA!!! THEY WILL BE SO EXCITED... AND THEN BAM!

KNOCK KNOCK.
WHO'S THERE?
NOOBIE.
NOOBIE WHO?
...... TBD

JXX

46YZ4178 337xPh1θ9G611st2

Chapter 9
I'M OVER IT

CutiePie55 ends the FaceTime call and mentions stopping by Child's house sometime later in the day to pick up the iPad. The mood has lightened considerably.

Child321654: Well that was hilarious! Best day ever!!! I still can't get over the name Basketcase87.

KSpicer333: I have got to meet CutiePie's grandma. Wouldn't it be hilarious to teach her how to play Roblox or Minecraft?

C: That would be amazeballs!!!

K: She could start her own YouTube channel! And we could be her guests.

C: Totally! Can you even imagine? Then it goes viral and we all end up on Ellen?

K: I love Ellen! That would be the best.

C: So, since the prank is off, want to play some Roblox?

K: Yeah, I guess so.

C: Really? Do you mean it? I thought you were totally going to say NO! I kind of actually said it as a joke.

K: I know, but I really miss it. AND now I'm feeling pretty good about that John Doe thing. It seems so dumb now that we've all talked about it. Who cares if someone is pulling an online prank on me? I'm sure you are right about CutiePie working with Brian again for April Fool's Day too. She seemed SO guilty!

C: I know, right? Why else would she have made a screenshot on the iPad?

K: So not like her. I mean what is the worst thing that could really happen anyways? John Doe is just a random person hacking accounts, not a ghost or something totally scary. Just some random person trying to hoax people and trying to get us believe in some dumb story. Someone's probably going to come out with a new "John Doe" game or something that costs 1,000 Robux and this is all just a big advertising ploy.

C: Totally! I mean, even if this is some dude that is a real hacker? So what? You might lose a few Robux, no big deal.

K: Exactly. Just Robux, nothing scary. I'm over it.

John Doe's Diary Entry #9:

Chapter 10
ALTER EGO

KSpicer333: What do you want to play first? A little Jail Break?

Child321654: I'm obsessed with that game!!! My mom can't stand when I play it though. Sometimes I get a little... um... stressed?!?

K: Shocker! You? Stressed at a game? So surprising!

C: Whatever! It's not like you are totally calm. Supergirlyscreamer!

K: What the what?

C: You know, when we play Murder Mystery 2 and you...

KSpicer cuts off Child: NO! My Roblox account. It says I've been banned!!! How can I be banned? I've hardly even played!!!

C: Banned for what?

K: I don't know, let me see if I can find out.

C: Maybe you've been sleep-playing and you've been bullying at midnight. HA!

K: You are just hilarious today.

C: Maybe you have been living in an alternate world and you are meanie McMeanerstein in that world. Your alter ego! (Starts laughing)

K: What the heck are even talking about? Alter ego?!?

C: MAYBE you have secretly been John Doe this whole time and this is just another one of your tricks! (ROFL)

K: Alright, you have completely lost it! Really? Just...REALLY?

Child continues to laugh hysterically while KSpicer begins to research why the account is banned.

K: Okay this is weird! It says that my account has been disabled for seven days.

C: For what?

K: I don't know, this all it says –

Our content monitors have determined that your behavior on ROBLOX has been in violation of our Terms of Service. We will terminate your account if you do not abide by the rules.

C: Huh? Well that's pretty vague!

K: Vague? What does that mean?

C: Seriously? It means when something isn't specific.

K: Oh, I guess I failed vocabulary. HA! Whatever.

C: So, when does it say you can you play?

K: Okay, that is even weirder! It says my account will be re-activated after April 7, 2017 at 3:33am.

C: Hey! It's your lucky number, 333.

K: Yeah, real lucky! I'm banned for a week!!!

C: A whole week? Bummer!!! How did that happen? Just use a guest account then.

K: This is super not cool! I can be a guest, but why was I banned in the first place?

C: I don't know, but I just realized that if you have been banned for EXACTLY seven days then wouldn't that mean that you had to have been playing at three in the morning today, on April Fool's?

K: I didn't play at three in the morning!!! I have never played at three in the morning! Well, except that one time...and technically it was four in the morning.

C: Well if it wasn't you playing, then who would be using your account? Who has your password?

K: Other than my parents, no one! And it isn't likely that my mom or dad would be up at three o-clock playing Roblox.

C: Make that a definite NO. Can you even imagine? Your mom playing on your account in the middle of the night? Doing such terrible things that she got you banned?

Child starts laughing.

K: Yeah, that would be funny and all if I didn't just think of this...

C: Of what? Your dad playing on your account and he stinks so bad at the game that it gets you banned? (Bursts out laughing even harder.)

K: Um, as hilarious as that is to even think about, I'm thinking this might be way worse.

C: (Through laughs) What...what...are you...talking...a...about? Whew! I just can't stop!!! This is SUCH a good day!

K: I'm reading up on getting randomly banned and it usually is because someone has hacked your account.

C: (Stops laughing) Wait, what? Are you serious?

K: Well nothing else makes any sense!

C: Okay, seriously? That is just pure meanness. Why would someone do that?

K: What if...

C: Ohhhh, maybe to use up your Robux? But that doesn't make sense since they would play as you. It's not like they can keep what they buy.

K: No, what if...

C: Uh huh, keep talking. Can't read minds...

K: That would require you to shush for a second! What if it is a more than just a random hacker?

C: Like a demon?

K: No!!!

C: Than what?

K: You mean who?

C: Huh?

K: What if it really is John Doe? What if he really is still after me?

John Doe's Diary Entry #10:

JOJOJOKER,

I'M TAKING DOWN THE SERVERS SOME DAY, ALL OF THE ROBLOX SERVERS. WONT THAT BE FUN?
ALL THEY WILL SEE IS ME. WHAT WOULD EVERYONE DO INSTEAD? MINECRAFT? NO!!! THAT'S OLD SCHOOL. I HAVE MY ULTIMATE PLAN IN MIND. I WILL SOON BE RICH...

BOO HOO SCAREDY CATS

JD

MY DRAWING STINKS!!!

Chapter 11
10,000 ROBUX

KSpicer and Child sit in silence for a few moments, thinking about what to do next.

Child321654: Um, I thought you gave up on that idea. That John Doe is real and all.

KSpicer333: Well whoever took over the John Doe account has to be a real person somewhere. And for whatever reason, he is after me!

C: A tad dramatic, but yes, that is seemingly kind of true.

K: Let's just say it is true for a minute. Isn't there some way to catch him in the act and at least report it to Roblox? Maybe they can actually catch this psycho so he will stop messing with people's games. And their lives...

C: I'm sure there has to be away.
Thinking....thinking...thinking... Let's record it!!! Like on FaceBook Live or even just a video capture so we can have proof.

K: Yes, of course! A vid! Not FB live though, because maybe nothing will happen. And then we would look really derpie.

C: True. Then we can just post the vid on YouTube if we catch him.

K: Totally! My dad has a tripod and I can set up my phone to capture.

C: Sweet!!! Let's do it!

KSpicer grabs the equipment and sets it up next to the desk area focusing in on the laptops.

C: Okay... now what? How are we supposed to catch John Doe in action when your account is banned?

K: Yeah, I kinda forgot about that part. Hmmm...

C: You could make a new account with something similar, like KSpicerBooty333.

K: Really?

C: Or what about KSpicerisababynoobiepants333 (starts laughing)

K: Uh huh, you are so super hilarious! And SO original. NOT.

C: Okay, I got it! What about KSpicerStinksatRoblox333? (bursts out laughing uncontrollably)

K: HELPFUL!!! (chuckling)

C: Ah man, can this day get any better?

K: Yes, it actually could! If I had my account back!!!

C: Oh yeah, right. That. True story.

K: Yeah, thanks for thinking of me and all.

C: Whoops! Sorry about that. Lol. Back to work here. Let's at least bring up my account on Roblox.

Child321654 sets her laptop next to KSpicer's and logs in. Looking over at KSpicer's laptop, Child notices something unusual.

C: Wait, you have over 10,000 Robux?

K: No, what are you talking about?

C: Look! On your screen, it says your account has exactly 11,320 Robux!

K: That can't be right! I've never had that much. I only have like 175 or something. And wait, how is my account showing if I've been banned?

C: Maybe you're unbanned!

K: I that a thing? Unbanned? Seriously though, this is weird. I was literally just banned! What the heck is going on?

C: And who bought you the Robux?

K: I have NO idea! I'm freaking out a little and yet at the same time I want to scream and dance that I have over TEN THOUSAND Robux!!!!

C: Lucky!

K: I'm totally lucky! Maybe I shouldn't spend them, maybe it is a glitch or something. I'm nervous. What if I get in trouble?

C: OMG! Take it down a notch. Freak out much?

K: Or maybe Roblox is doing this on purpose and giving all of us an awesome April Fools Day present!

C: Then you better hurry and use those Robux before they take them away.

K: Ooooo, good point!

C: Um, shouldn't we be recording all this? You know, just in case?

K: Oh geez! I totally spaced on that! Where is the remote? I'll turn it on.

C: Here...wait!

K: For what?

C: Shouldn't we come up with a cool intro for when we post this to YouTube?

K: Oh right! Okay, I'll say my normal intro and then I'll introduce you. Then we can fill them in on what we are doing.

C: What are we doing?

K: Trying to catch John Doe, remember? DUH!!!

C: I know that! I just meant, don't we need a plan or something?

K: Nope! Now that I'm in again, let's just start playing. If he is really out to get me, he will show up. Then BAM! We will have proof!

C: Still a little confused on what that will do for us, but I'll roll with it. I really don't get how you are unbanned suddenly.

K: Me neither! But I've got a zillion Robux, so who cares? Let's do this! 3...2...1... "Hey everyone, it's KSpicer333..."

Video recording starts.

John Doe's Diary Entry #11:

J'ADY BOY

BEST DAY EVER

THIS IS THE BEGINNING
OF DOMINATION! THEY ARE
TAKING THE BAIT JUST
LIKE HUNGRY GUPPIES.

YESSS

√TING G6^3 IN
5 MINUTES

HISTORY

JD

Chapter 12
BACON HAIR

Ten minutes later, KSpicer stops the recording.

Child321654: Hey! What are you doing?

KSpicer333: Nothing has happened yet, so I thought I would start over.

C: What do you mean nothing has happened? We were just epic at Jail Break!!!

K: Yeah, I know, but I can post that as a separate video. We're trying to catch John Doe in the act, remember?

C: Oh that! HA! That was so fun that I almost forgot.

K: Um really?

C: Lol. So, start the next one and let's go play something different. What about Murder Mystery 2?

K: Ugh.

C: What ugh? You love that game!!!

K: LOVED it you mean.

C: Oh, come on!!! You still love it and you know it. If the goal is to catch John Doe, then what better game to play?

K: I know, it just makes me all jittery.

C: Jittery?

K: Like all EHH inside when I play.

C: Huh?

K: Okay fine! I get stressed out when I play!

C: Wait, you make fun of ME for getting stressed out playing that game. What the heck?

K: Well that's because you used to cry and run in the other room when you got murdered!!!

C: Did not!

K: Uh, yeah. Yeah you did! Baby McScotchy pants.

C: Baby McScotchy pants?!? That's actually a good one. I'm using it.

K: Okay let's do this then.

C: Really?

K: Yeah. I'm ready to go for it.

C: YES! Ready JD? Here we come! Watch out for little baby noobie pants and baby McScotchy pants!!!

KSpicer and Child laugh nervously as they enter the game.

C: You forgot to start the recording!

K: I'll start it once we are in.

C: K.

K: Hey look! Its TyFighter. He's in our game!

C: Awesome, now start the recording.

K: Oh yeah. (Starts recording.) "Hey guys, it's KSpicer333 here with Child321654. We are back in Murder Mystery 2 for the final battle."

C: Final battle?

K: Sounds epic right?

C: Oh I get it! Because of the John Doe thing.

K: DUH! So everyone, we are out to catch John Doe tonight and what better place to do that than in MM2? Everyone ready?

C: Let's do this! Ahhhhhh man, I'm innocent! Shooty booty.

K: Woo hoo! I'm sheriff. Oh yeah, I'm sheriff and I'm going to rage on the murderer. Let me know if you see who it is.

C: K. Oh hey, there's Tyfighter! Uh oh dude, you better run!!! (Slash sound.) Well that happened.

K: Oh boy, Ty is dead. Bummer. Who's the murderer?

C: Some guy with bacon hair.

K: Noob.

C: Prob.

K: What's his name?

C: Not sure yet. But I'm hiding in my regular spot.

K: He has hardly killed anyone. What is he doing? Just standing around or something?

C: Don't know, don't care. Just hiding.

K: K. I'm on the hunt. Let me know if you see anything.

C: Seriously, this guy must be a total noob. The time is almost up!

K: Yeah and there are all these people with me standing outside. If he came out here, he could go on a rampage.

C: Clock is ticking – Innocents are going to win this round.

K: Yep. Seriously, this is just dumb. Did he go AFK or something? Why did this have to happen when I was sheriff? Such a waste!

C: I know, right. 3....2.... (suddenly Screams and flies off the chair.)

John Doe's Diary Entry #12:

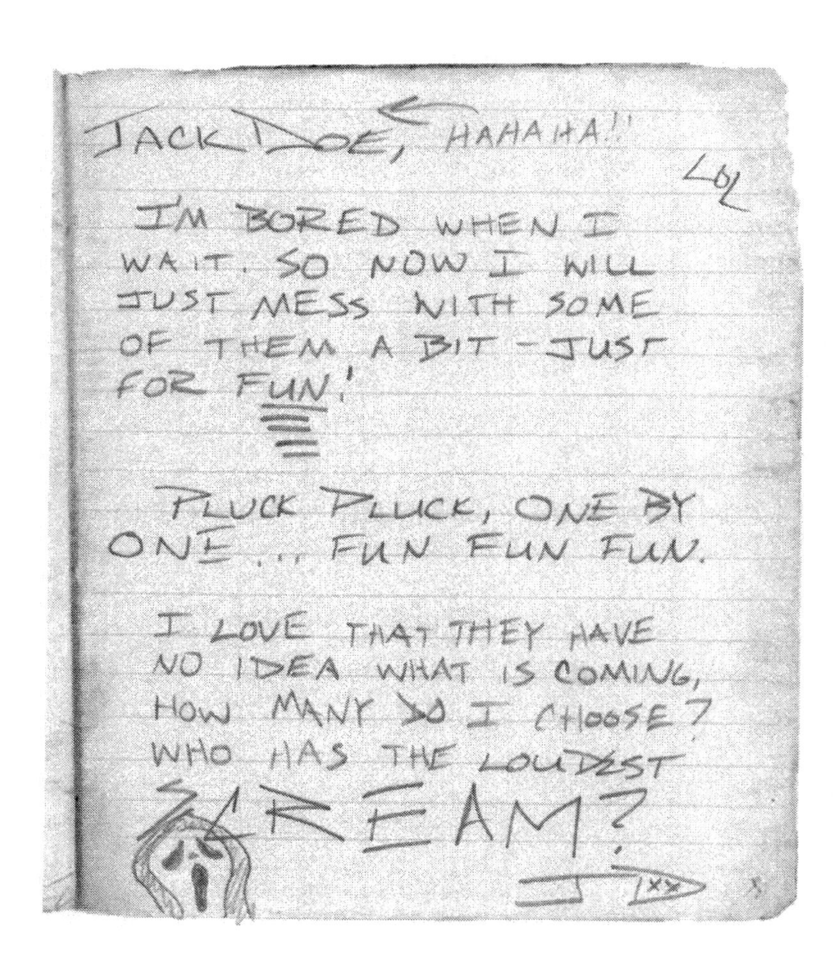
JACK DOE, HAHAHA!!

LOL

I'M BORED WHEN I WAIT. SO NOW I WILL JUST MESS WITH SOME OF THEM A BIT - JUST FOR FUN!

PLUCK PLUCK, ONE BY ONE... FUN FUN FUN.

I LOVE THAT THEY HAVE NO IDEA WHAT IS COMING, HOW MANY DO I CHOOSE? WHO HAS THE LOUDEST SCREAM?

J D xx

Chapter 13
GUEST WHO?

KSpicer333: What happened? You scared me!!!!

Child321654: Scared you? Bacon hair killed me at the last minute and scared me!!! I have no idea where he came from either!

KSpicer snorts and starts laughing, almost knocking the mouse off the desk.

C: It's not THAT funny! Geez. My heart is racing. What the heck?

K: You should have seen yourself!!! It was hilarious! HAAAAAAAA! And we have it on video!

C: Oh great. What did I look like?

K: You had this face! HAAAA! And then you were like in slow motion flying off the chair. Ah man, you have got to see that. But let's play another round first, okay?

C: Not sure about this. I think I will just be AFK and just watch. I'm a mess now.

K: Why yes, yes you are.

C: Thanks, just thanks.

K: Just telling it like it is. You are witnessing this people! Can't wait to hear what you think of Child's fall. Leave a comment below of how dumb it looked.

C: Really, you're going there?

K: Just did!

C: I think bacon hair is Thinktank2020. See him in the corner?

K: Yeah, just a noob.

C: Game is about to start. Come on baby, let me be the murderer!

K: I thought you were going to be AFK.

C: Changed my mind.

K: Wait, am I reading that right? Is that Guest666 on the list?

C: WHAT?!? OMG! It totally is!

K: No way! This is awesome!

C: Could just be another April Fool's thing or something.

K: What does he look like?

C: Dunno. Didn't see before we got pulled in. Ah man, innocent again.

K: Me too. I'm kind of nervous and excited. I'm nervouscited.

C: Me too. Love the hotel map. Don't go in...(gets cut off mid-sentence.)

K: The theater, yeah, you say that every single time we play.

C: I do?

K: Yes, you do.

C: Oops, sorry about that.

K: No biggie.

C: Look, how creepy! There's Guest666!!! He is all black and just standing in the fountain.

K: Awkward.

C: Awkwardly creepy. I'm outie. Headed upstairs to spectate from my normal spot.

K: I'm with you.

C: What the heck? He's just standing there.

K: He has to be the murderer. Otherwise he would be hiding, right?

C: I'm thinking so.

K: Wait, this map isn't right.

C: What? You're right. There wasn't black on the floor before. Maybe they changed it.

K: Weird.

C: Look, he's hopping in the fountain now. I wonder if this is the real Guest666?

K: I don't know, but I'm starting to freak out a little.

Chat pops up:

Guest666: No one will make it out alive.

C: What the what? What a dork. What is he even talking about?

K: Who's the sheriff? Get him you fool!

C: If he's the murderer, why isn't he going after anyone?

K: I don't know, but this is kinda dumb but still creeping me out.

C: The game only has a few seconds left.

Guest666 in chat: Goodbye.

C: See ya punk!

Just then, both KSpicer and Child die in the game from the murderer, Guest666. They both scream and jump back from the desk.

K: What the...who the...what just happened?

C: How did we die? And at the same time?

K: And from Guest666? He was in the fountain!

C: LOOK! It shows that everyone died!!!

K: I'm out. (Leaves game.)

C: Yep. Me too. (Leaves game.) That was WAY too freaky!!!

K: That just isn't even possible! How did he do that? I don't get it.

C: Oooo, we are still recording! We'll have to watch that again later. Did you catch that people? All of us were murdered at the same time! Not possible? Well guess again. It is if Guest666 is in your game.

K: Crazy town. This has to be a Roblox thing for today. Right? Let's play something lighter for a minute so I can stop shaking.

C: Good idea!

K: Okay everyone, thanks for watching this episode. We will start a second recording of our John Doe hunt in just a minute, so be sure to Subscribe and leave a Like. Thanks for watching! Bye!

C: See ya!

KSpicer stops the recording and they both sit silent for a moment to regain themselves.

C: Well, are you up for another round?

K: Let's start with a different game first and then go back in. I just need a minute.

C: Yeah, me too.

John Doe's Diary Entry #13:

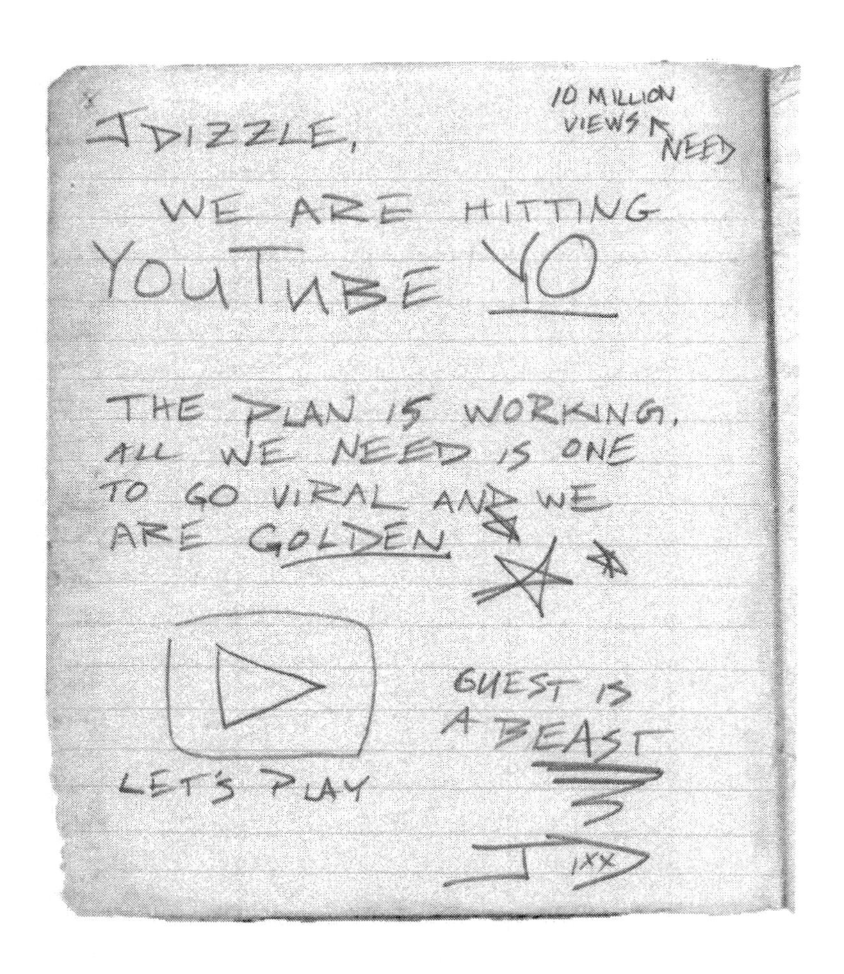

10 MILLION VIEWS NEED

JDIZZLE,

WE ARE HITTING YOUTUBE YO

THE PLAN IS WORKING. ALL WE NEED IS ONE TO GO VIRAL AND WE ARE GOLDEN

GUEST IS A BEAST

LET'S PLAY

J IXX

Chapter 14
NOT SO FRIEND REQUEST

KSpicer starts the recording again and gives the normal intro.

KSpicer333: Okay everyone, this is the second episode of the 'Hunting John Doe' series. Hope you enjoyed the first one and if you didn't see it, you are really missing out on Child flying off the chair!

Child321654: Yeah, that was pretty hilarious. I still have to see what I looked like.

K: WAY too funny. And there was the Guest666 thing...

C: Um, yeah, there was that. You have GOT to see that!!! Yes people, we did say Guest666. And you won't even believe what happened! This is going to go viral. I'm just sayin'. It really is that epic!

K: Sooo, first we are going to play some Meeps for a few minutes to calm our nerves and then back to another round of MM2. If you want to see the first episode, the link is down below. We are hoping for some more April Fool's Day action!

C: Ahhhhh, look at my Mimi. Isn't she cute?

K: You changed her into a little devil.

C: I know, cute right?

K: I like it! Let's see, what have they added since I was last here?

C: All sorts of new stuff to buy. When is the last time you watered your plants?

K: It's been forever...I'm sure they are a wilted mess. HA!

C: You know they don't really wilt, right?

K: I know. I was just kidding.

C: I'm headed into the store.

K: I'm going fishing. I need some cash to buy stuff first. Hmm, I don't remember that happening before.

C: What?

K: Well it just turned to night and for some reason it is really extra dark. I mean so dark that I can hardly see anything.

C: Huh? Let me go back outside.

K: See?

C: That is weird! This definitely didn't happen before. Must be new but I don't like it. I can hardly see in front of me. Like only a few steps. Where are you?

K: Still near the fishing pond. I'll stay here, come find me.

C: If this doesn't turn light soon, I'm outta here. This is lamo. I literally can't see a thing.

K: IKR? Super annoying. Hey! Did you see that?

C: Yeah, it was like a flash, like lightening or something.

K: Nope, this is not a cool update people. Not happy. We may have to switch games. Want to stop the recording?

C: Holy what the nuts?

K: What? What's wrong?

C: Turn around!

K: What in the what? It's Guest666 again!!!

C: And he's hopping in the pond! What is with this guy and water? We are totally not stopping the recording now.

K: This has GOT to be some Roblox hoax, right? I mean two games in a row? How likely is that?

C: What is going on?

K: Nope. Just nope. I'm out. I just can't. (Leaves game.) Sorry people! Just getting a little too weird.

C: I'm out too. (Leaves game.) It really would be a funny prank for the Roblox people to do this in every game, if that's what's happening. But IS that what is happening?

Child turns towards the camera.

C: What do you think people? Is this the most epic prank ever pulled on Roblox players or what? Comment below.

K: I'm hoping this isn't happening just to us.

C: No way! That would be completely unlikely. Let's try another game.

K: Like a Tycoon or something. Something super small with only a few players. Then we prove it was just a coincidence.

C: Right. What about Lumber Tycoon or Tix Factory?

K: Lumber it is!

C: Alright everyone, here we go!

KSpicer and Child get into the game.

K: Cool, it is just us and Bobsledfred7428. Bob sled Fred? What the heck? So hilarious!!!

C: So dumb. What kind of name is that?

K: Who knows? All I know is that he is not Guest666.

C: Right? Hey, go check if TyFighter is still on. Maybe he can join us.

K: K. (Switches screens to check friend status.) Ummmmmm, this is creepy. Check your friend requests.

C: Why? What?

K: I have a new friend request from Guest666. I'm guessing we all do. Go check!

C: Okay, that is just bizarre! And super amazingly creepy. And potentially AWESOME!!! Hmmmm, nope no request on mine. Not yet.

K: Well maybe it's coming. I'm sure everyone is getting one that was in the game.

C: You should accept it.

K: NOOOOOOOO! Not happening.

C: Come on, do it! Maybe he will lead us to John Doe.

K: Do you really think that two hackers are friends in real life?

C: Who knows? But maybe it could happen. Anything is possible!

K: Is it there yet?

C: What?

K: The friend request.

C: OH!!! Let me check again... nope. Nothing. It's just you.

K: Funny. I doubt it's just me.

C: Seems like it.

K: Nice. Real nice.

C: I'm just sayin'.

K: Such a good friend to me...

C: Oh NO!

K: Did you get the friend request?

C: No! It's HIM again.

K: WHAT? GUEST666?

C: No, that FreakBoy guy. He just joined the game. He is the absolute worst!

K: Don't do that! You scared me!!!

C: Oh sorry. It's just that FreakBoy was the one that just kept killing me over and over in that tycoon and I couldn't do anything. Remember? So super annoying.

K: Geez. I thought Guest666 joined or something. Don't freak me out.

C: It's just that he is so mean! FreakBoy is just the worst.

K: Really?

C: Uhhhh, triple UH OH!!!

K: Now what?

C: Or should I say hexa uh oh. Get it hexa, six?

K: OMG!!!

C: Too soon for the hexa jokes?

Child points at the screen showing that Guest666 joined the game.

John Doe's Diary Entry #14:

JJ,

I HAVE ONE WORD FOR YOU. CAN YOU SAY

GULLIBLE?

LOOK THAT ONE UP JACK. THE ROBUX TRICK IS BRILLIANT! WISH I HAD THOUGHT OF IT EARLIER. IT'S LIKE CANDY TO A BABY.

GET READY... HERE I COME.

IM THE INTERNET GANGSTER

JJxx

OUT

Chapter 15
GOTCHA

KSpicer333: Not again!!!

Child321654: I'm starting to think this might be just us and I'm freaking out a little inside.

K: Um, yeah, ya think? Text Tyler and see if this is happening in his games.

C: You mean TyFighter. (Nodding to the video capture.)

K: Yes, TyFighter, I mean. Totally. Sorry about that. Not really thinking straight right now.

C: Okay TyFighter, give me some good news... This has got to be going on all through Roblox today. Right? Come on...answer me.

K: Please, please, please...I'm crossing fingers and toes here.

C: How do you cross your toes?

K: I dunno, just sayin'. I want all the help I can get.

C: Well I'm crossing my legs, does that count?

K: I guess we will find out.

C: Ugh! Not answering. Let's FaceTime him.

K: K.

Facetime call to TyFighter. He picks up.

TyFighter: Can't talk, in Bed Wars. Really intense right now!

C: Fine.

K: Has Guest666 been joining your games?

T: What? What do you mean? What are you talking about?

K: I'll take that as a no.

C: Were you still in MM2 when Guest666 came in?

T: I don't think so. I left during the first game with you guys, when that bacon hair noob got me.

K: Shoot. Yeah, he was an odd one.

T: Wait did you say Guest666? Like the hacker? Like the real account?

C: Who knows. That's the account that came up, but we think it might be an April Fool's Day hoax or something.

K: We are HOPING that's what it is.

C: Ummmm, look!

T: What?

C: Not you, KSpicer!

K: OMG!!! Ty, we gotta go.

T: Why? WAIT! What's going on?

KSpicer ends the FaceTime abruptly.

K: This is nuts!!! How is this possible? What is going on?

C: I don't really know, but I'm SO excited that this is all being recorded!

K: Oh yeah! This is going to go viral!!!

C: Big shocker, Guest666 is just standing there. Now he's hopping again. What is with this guy? Is he like the Easter Bunny or something?

K: Lol. If I wasn't also terrified, I'd laugh at that.

C: Right?

John Doe enters the game.

K: OH NO OH NO OH NO!!!

C: I knew it!!! They are working together! Hacker buddies. HA! Is everyone seeing this?

K: I gotta jump. I can't do this.

C: YES, you can. Calm down! What is the worst that could happen? Remember? We went over this.

K: Okay, talk me down. Where is he? What is he going to do? I want to close my eyes. Need any food? I can go grab something. (Starts to get up.)

C: NO! We are doing this. Let's just get it over with!

K: Oh boy oh boy oh boy. Why are you so calm?

C: I’m not! I can just manage my stress better.

K: Oh really? You are so dumb right now.

John Doe in Chat: Gotcha

Kspicer screams and leaves the game. Child leaves the game just after.

John Doe's Diary Entry #15:

JPOP,

$$$ ON MY MIND

BOO!

* KEEP THESE CODES WORKING AND SEE HOW MANY WE GET.

WHY ARE THEY SO DUMB?

WHO CARES!!!

SO FAR WE ARE AT 32. ERASE OUR PATH BY MID.

J IXX

SO DUMB SO SO SO DUMB

Chapter 16
GAME CRASHERS

Child321654: What did you do that for?

KSpicer333: I'm sorry! I freaked out!!! What do you want me to do?

C: Stay in and see what happens...you know? The plan?

K: That was just too much. What does "gotcha" mean? Was he going to GET me? How would he get me? What does get me do?

C: He didn't say "gotcha KSpicer," so calm down!

K: So why did you leave then? You could have stayed in to see what happened.

C: Alone? No way! NO thank you. Plus, he is after you, not me. (Snickers.)

K: OH NICE! Thanks a lot for all your reassurance. I'm feeling SO much better. Good friend you are!

C: I was just joking. Maybe it is still a Roblox hoax. Let's go into something else and see what happens.

K: I don't know if I can do this anymore. This was fun at first, but now it is all too real.

C: Just one more game...please? Or are you a stinky baby noobie that still sucks on a binky? (Makes a sucking noise.)

K: Seriously? Right now? This is completely serious.

C: Just trying to keep it light.

K: Uh huh. Not helping. We are still recording you know.

C: Yep!

K: Fine!!! One last game and then we stop and cut the recording. I'm done for the night. Promise?

C: Promise! People, we are doing this! Are you all ready to catch the real John Doe? Famous Roblox Hacker of the stars.

K: Of the stars?

C: I have no idea. It just came out.

K: WAIT!!!

C: Wha?

K: My Robux are gone!!! My precious Robux!!! My fresh new 10,000 Robux that I was going to use to buy that amazing hair I've been wanting!

C: Maybe that's what JD meant by "gotcha."

K: OMG! He is after me! It had to be him!!! The real him. John Doe stole my Robux!!!

C: Well, technically they weren't really your Robux.

K: True, but he still stole them! It had to be him.

C: Maybe he's the one that gave them to you in the first place.

K: What? Why would he do that? How does that even make sense?

C: Maybe he is messing with you. You know, gave you some bait to start playing Roblox again?

K: Really? That seems pretty unbelievable.

C: Not as unbelievable as him going after you in the *first place*. But that IS happening, so this kinda makes sense.

K: I can't go back in now!

C: Since there is nothing left to steal, what else could he do? Nothing. I don't think. Let's go into a game and find out. Come on!

K: FINE! That's it, I've had it with this guy. Let's do it.

C: What about Normal Elevator?

K: Are you kidding me? Totally no! Too scary right now. Can you even imagine what could go wrong there?

C: True. Tornado Simulator?

K: Huh? Is that a thing?

C: Yeah!!! It's fun.

K: I know, what about Airplane Simulator?

C: Why do you like that game so much?

K: I don't know! It is so fun!

C: You can't do ANYTHING in there.

K: Yes, you can. They have new stuff.

C: Uh huh. But can you do anything or do you still just sit around with your coffee and newspaper?

K: The new stuff makes it WAY more fun.

C: Fine. Just go in.

Child and KSpicer join the game.

K: Sweet! We got in together.

C: Ugh, this is so dumb. Too many people are trying to get downstairs. What is down there anyway?

K: It's cool; it's the lounge area.

C: So, you just stand around? But downstairs instead?

K: Pretty much, but it is fun.

C: Sounds amazing. (Sarcastically.)

K: Wait, my VIP isn't working. I can't go into the cockpit. NOT cool.

C: Ummm, are you showing other people in there? The group around me literally just disappeared. Is the game glitching?

K: No, I see people...look on my screen. No wait, they are gone. Can I see you?

C: I don't know, but I see one familiar face...

K: Ty?

C: JOHN DOE!!!!

John Doe in the Chat: BOO!

K: AHHHHHHHH!!!

C: Stay IN – DON'T move a muscle.

K: Couldn't if I tried – I'm frozen. Literally frozen.

Across the screen: Game Lost Connection.

K: Whew. Thank goodness! That was good timing.

C: Or was that John Doe? Do you think maybe HE crashed the game?

K: Maybe. Who knows. All I know is that I'm done with this tonight. I cannot take it anymore.

C: Wait, let's just see if it lets us in and if everything is normal. Then we can go right out. I just gotta know if it crashed on its own or not.

K: How is going back in going to tell you that?

C: Good point, but if John Doe reappears, I promise we will be out for the night.

K: Okay FINE! But this is it! Pinky promise me!!!

C: Pinky promise.

John Doe's Diary Entry #16:

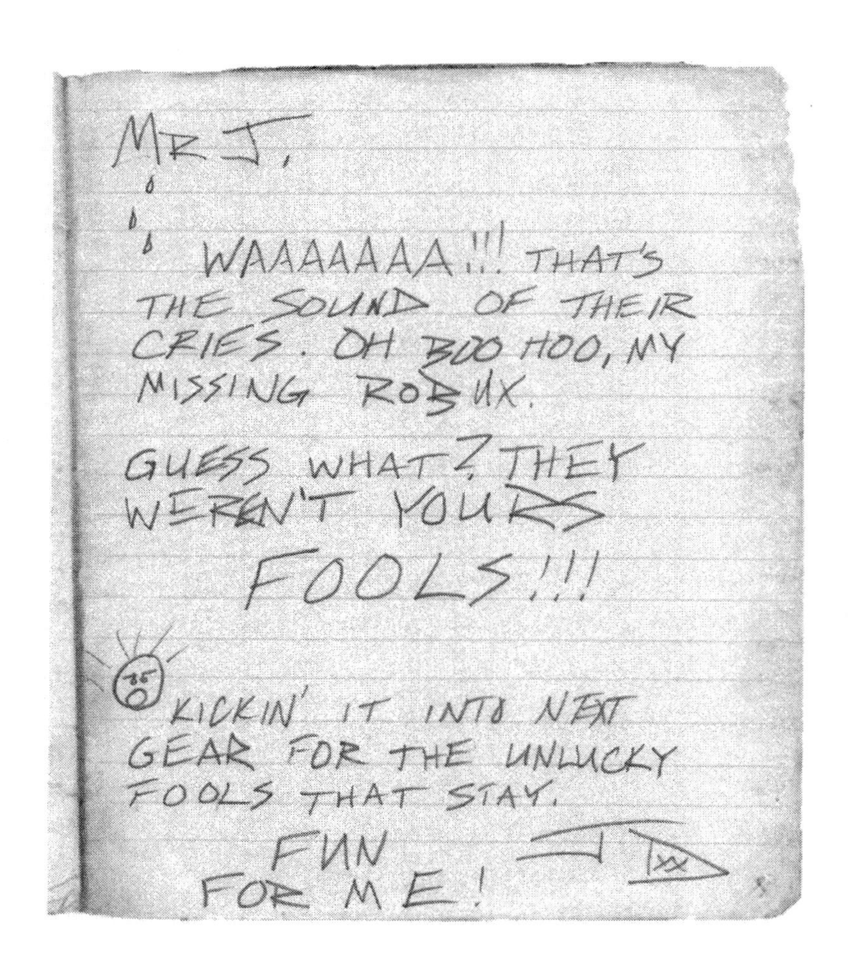

MR J,

WAAAAAAA!!! THAT'S
THE SOUND OF THEIR
CRIES. OH BOO HOO, MY
MISSING ROBUX.

GUESS WHAT? THEY
WEREN'T YOURS

FOOLS!!!

KICKIN' IT INTO NEXT
GEAR FOR THE UNLUCKY
FOOLS THAT STAY.

FUN
FOR ME!

JD

Chapter 17
THE REAL DEAL

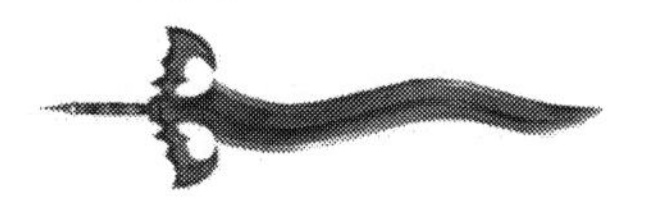

KSpicer and Child join the game one last time.

KSpicer333: Here goes nothin'.

Child321654: Huh?

K: I don't know. My dad says that whenever we try something new.

C: Your dad says weird stuff sometimes.

K: Yeah. But sometimes it's catchy!

C: True. Okay, so things seem kinda normal.

K: You spoke too soon!!! I can't move. Nothing is working. Look! (Bangs on keyboard and mouse.)

C: Calm down! I think it's just going to crash again. The game must be having problems.

K: Okay, well I think you have proved your point now. Let's...

John Doe joins the game.

John Doe in the chat: Watch out KSpicer

K: WHAAAAAAAAAAAA?!?!?!?

The game loses connection again. Neither of them say a word. Just then, there is a loud knock at the back door. Both Child and KSpicer scream and jump out of their chairs.

K: OMG!!! What are we going to do? Do you think it's John Doe?

C: No, that would be CRAZY!!! No way no way! He's not real!!

K: Okay, let's calm down and think about it. Go answer the door.

C: NO! YOU answer the door.

K: You said that John Doe isn't real, so why are you scared?

C: Because what if it is?

K: I knew it!

C: So?

Knock knock knock...even harder than before.

C: Maybe he will go away.

K: Yeah, maybe. We should hide, turn off the lights or something.

C: Kinda too late for that! Then he would really know we are in here.

K: True. What are we going to do?

C: I don't know! Where is your mom?

K: At the neighbor's house.

C: Let's text her.

K: And say what, "Help! John Doe is at the door to come get me?"

C: Sounds kinda dumb when you say it like that.

KNOCK KNOCK KNOCK!

John Doe's Diary Entry #17:

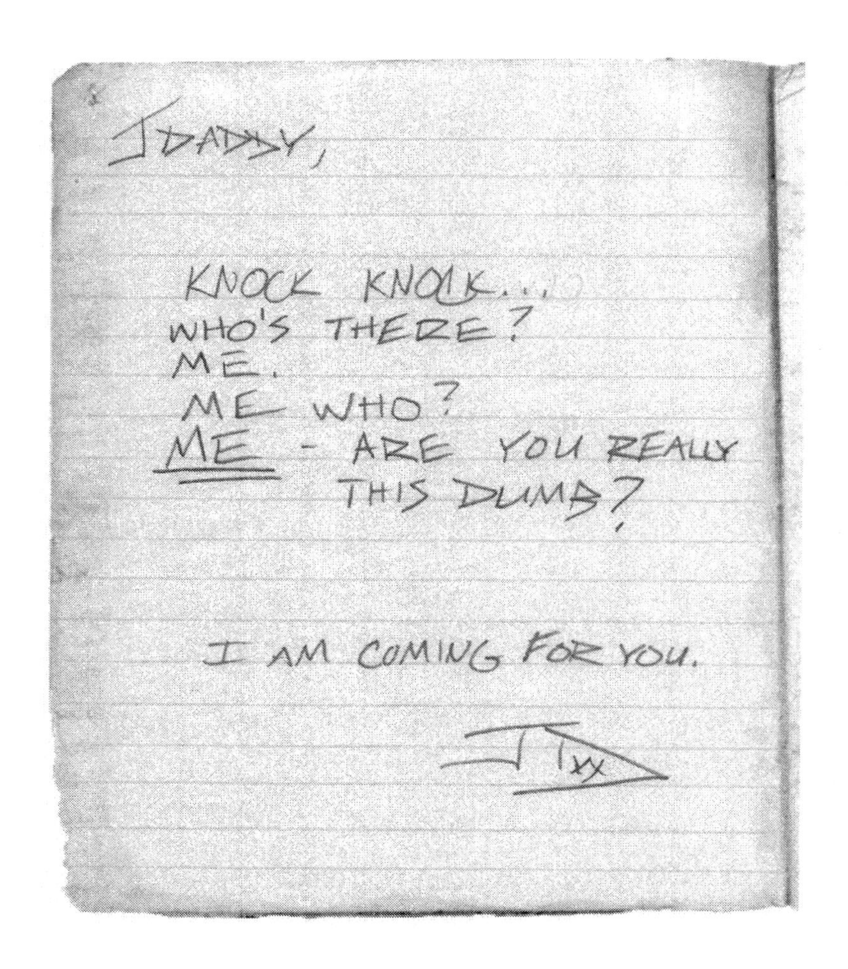
JDADDY,

KNOCK KNOCK...
WHO'S THERE?
ME.
ME WHO?
ME - ARE YOU REALLY
THIS DUMB?

I AM COMING FOR YOU.

JTxx

Chapter 18
RECORDED

Voice from Outside: Hey K! Let us in! We know you're there.

Child looks up confused.

KSpicer333: Its CutiePie!!! (Huge gasp and runs to the door.)

KSpicer sees CutiePie and her cousin Brian standing in the courtyard peering in.

K: What a relief to see you guys!

C: Yeah, what a HUGE relief!

CutiePie55: What's going on? What took you so long to answer the door?

C: Oh nothing. We just thought you were John Doe.

KSpicer notices Brian start to laugh.

CP: John Doe? Not that again? It's been like weeks!

K: Well it WAS weeks until tonight.

C: Have you been on Roblox at all today?

CP: No, we had a big family thing. Brian drove me home and I was trying to find you guys so I could get my iPad.

K: Well, just so you know, John Doe is officially stalking ME! It is the truth!

Brian: (Laughs out loud) Really? John Doe is after you again?

C: Its true!

B: Ahhhh. okay.

K: Seriously! We thought Roblox was just playing an April Fool's hoax on all its users today, but then it just got personal.

CutiePie and Brian exchange looks.

C: We have proof!!!

CP: You do? How?

K: We recorded the WHOLE thing!

C: Yeah, we have it all on video. Maybe we can get famous by exposing the biggest hacker known in history!

B: I sincerely doubt that John Doe is the biggest hacker in history. What has he even done? It's not like he hacked into the Pentagon or something.

C: Well, whatever! It's still going to be huge when we release it.

CP: I want to see it!

K: Okay, let me show you.

KSpicer grabs the phone off the tripod to show the group.

K: What the heck? The phone is dead!!!

C: You have GOT to be kidding me!

K: I swear we have the whole thing recorded! Something happened.

B: What, like did John Doe hack your phone too? (Starts laughing.)

CutiePie joins in the laughter.

K: What is with you two? I'm sure I have most of it recorded. Once I charge it back up, you'll see! It was completely charged when we started. So bizarre; I don't get it.

C: Wait, you guys keep looking at each other weird. Did you have something to do with all this?

B: Nope, nothing.

CP: How could we? We were with our family? (Still smiling and looks over at Brian.)

K: Hmmm, something seems fishy with you two. Is this your big April Fool's Day joke on us? Is that what's going on?

C: Wait a minute! Is it? Where were you really today? Were you together pulling another John Doe hacker prank on us?

B: Why would I waste my time messing with you?

K: Really?

C: Very funny guys! This was over the top. And how come you did it to both of us? Cutie, how come you didn't clue me in this morning?

CP: What are you even talking about?

K: That's it. I'm banning you from my Minecraft server for a week. Maybe even a month. Or maybe forever!

C: I don't even like either of you right now.

K: Me either.

B: You two must have eaten too much candy today. There is some crazy talk going on up in here.

C: Look who you're calling crazy! Who would do this to two innocent kids.

B: Innocent?

K: Yeah! What did we ever do to you?

Brian shakes his head, still with a smirk on his face and walks towards the door.

B: Whatever, I'm out. See ya!

John Doe's Diary Entry #18:

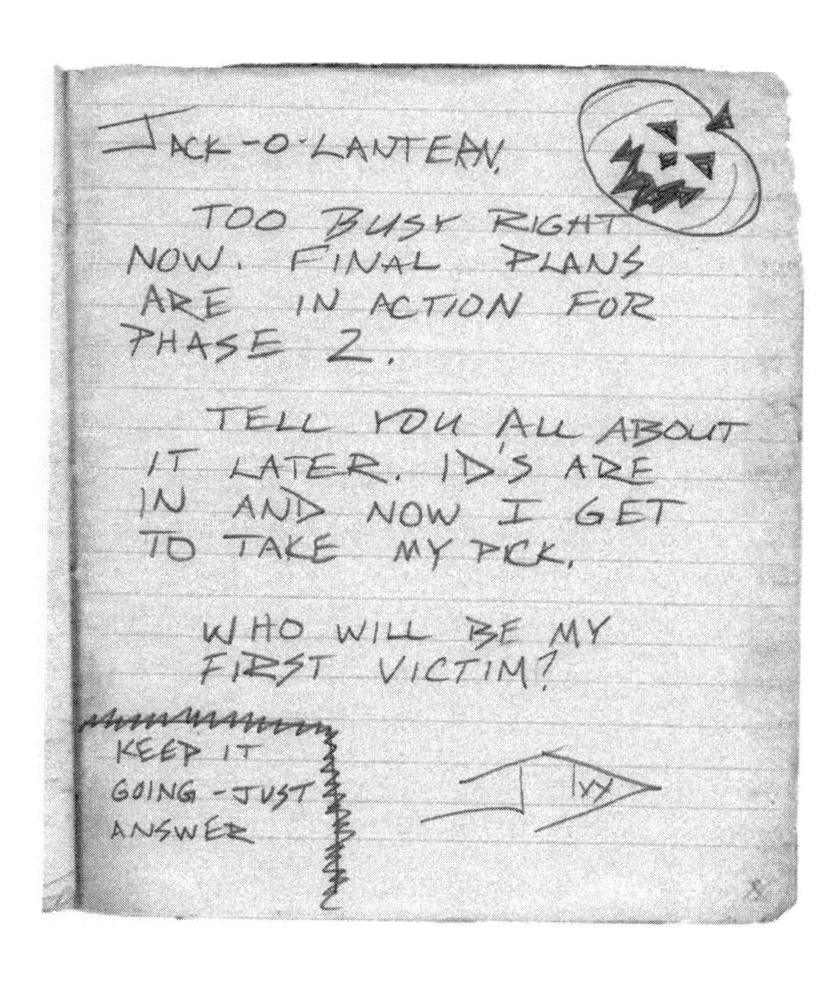
JACK-O-LANTERN.

TOO BUSY RIGHT NOW. FINAL PLANS ARE IN ACTION FOR PHASE 2.

TELL YOU ALL ABOUT IT LATER. ID'S ARE IN AND NOW I GET TO TAKE MY PICK.

WHO WILL BE MY FIRST VICTIM?

KEEP IT GOING - JUST ANSWER

Chapter 19
NO ANSWER

CP: I have no idea what is going on here, but I need to get my iPad.

C: It's still at my house. KSpicer, I better go anyways. CutiePie, I'll walk with you to my house and you can get your iPad.

CP: Thanks.

K: You're just going to leave me like this?

C: The hoax is over! We found the real hackers. It was just one big dumb mean April Fool's Day joke. So, nothing to freak out about anymore. Next year, remind me to go out of town on April 1st. This was exhausting.

CP: You are crazy! I had nothing to do with it. I swear!

K: Uh huh, just like always.

CutiePie rolls her eyes and starts to follow Brian. All four walk out the back door together.

K: Well thanks Child for an interesting day. I guess.

C: Yeah, you too! I still think we should post those videos tomorrow. We may still get famous.

K: I really hope we got most of it captured. Then maybe this nightmare experience would at least feel worth it.

KSpicer hears a FaceTime call from the other room.

K: I should probably get that. It's probably Tyler wondering why we hung up so fast.

C: Oh yeah! I totally forgot about him. LOL. Whoops, sorry not sorry TyFighter.

K: Later guys.

Brian, CutiePie and Child say goodbye and head out to the street. KSpicer goes back into the bedroom where the FaceTime call stops. KSpicer plops down onto the desk chair, stares up at the ceiling and takes a loud deep breath. FaceTime call starts again.

K: Sorry Tyler, you're just going to have to wait until tomorrow. I'm too exhausted. (Puts face in hands.)

FaceTime finally stops.

KSpicer looks up at the laptop, ready to close it all down for the night and hears a "ping" from the Roblox chat.

K: Huh? Tyler, I just can't talk… (opens chat.)

FaceTime rings again.

John Doe in Chat: Answer…It's me

KSpicer spins around in the chair and looks at the iPad:

Incoming FaceTime from Unknown Caller.

John Doe's Diary Entry #19:

To Be Continued (again)...

What is John Doe's Master Plan? Check out Amazon.com for Volume 3 and join our list at www.kspicer.com. Subscribe to K*Spicer's YouTube channel and you can be the first to know about new book releases and where to purchase. Hope you enjoyed it!

Turn the page for more vital info...

Want to know what happens next? More books are on the way! Join our list at www.kspicer.com to be the first to hear about the next book release, upcoming contests and other fun gaming awesomeness. We would love to hear from you about the book series, so make sure you subscribe to our YouTube channels and chat with us.

Check out K*Spicer's YouTube channel – KSpicer, the channel, has just begun. Watch some Roblox and Minecraft game play as well as book trailers and soon to include Sims4 gaming!

Check out LittleWalker's YouTube channel – Littlewalker08plays, for gaming, gymnastics and super random friend challenges. One never knows what exciting videos are being uploaded next! She can also be found under the Roblox username Child321654 – the same one in this book! Let her know if you hop in the same game and she might just give you a shout out.

Authors:

K*Spicer – Who is the real K*Spicer? Check out the YouTube channels to find out more. Oh and yes, K*Spicer loves both Roblox and Minecraft equally.

LittleWalker – Little Walker is K*Spicer's number one gaming friend. Although LittleWalker is school aged, she is a main contributor to the subject matter of the Roblox Hacker Diaries. Without her, K*Spicer would never have found her passion for gaming. Is there more to K*Spicer and Littlewalker's relationship? Subcribe and stay tuned to either YouTube channel to learn more about them.

Made in the USA
San Bernardino, CA
11 February 2018